HOME ALONE 2
LOST IN NEW YORK
ACTIVITY BOOK

Written by Joanne Mattern
From the screenplay by John Hughes

Illustrated by Roy Schlemme

Troll Associates

TWENTIETH CENTURY FOX PRESENTS A JOHN HUGHES PRODUCTION A CHRIS COLUMBUS FILM
MACAULAY CULKIN JOE PESCI DANIEL STERN JOHN HEARD HOME ALONE 2 TIM CURRY BRENDA FRICKER
AND CATHERINE O'HARA MUSIC BY JOHN WILLIAMS EDITOR RAJA GOSNELL PRODUCTION DESIGNER SANDY VENEZIANO
DIRECTOR OF PHOTOGRAPHY JULIO MACAT EXECUTIVE PRODUCERS MARK RADCLIFFE DUNCAN HENDERSON RICHARD VANE
WRITTEN AND PRODUCED BY JOHN HUGHES DIRECTED BY CHRIS COLUMBUS

Color by DELUXE ®
© 1992 TWENTIETH CENTURY FOX

Soundtrack available on Fox Records

McCallister Family Word Search

The McCallisters are all going to Florida for Christmas. Can you find all the members of this large family in this word-search puzzle? Look across, up and down, and diagonally.

BROOKE   **LESLIE**
BUZZ   **LINNIE**
FRANK   **MEGAN**
FULLER   **PETER**
JEFF   **ROD**
KATE   **SONDRA**
KEVIN   **TRACEY**

```
F L H X D R Q N F S I C
J R I L E S L I E F F N
A T O G P E T E B E U E
K T S D O N K J R V L L
Y R B U Z Z A F O Q L V
V A F K O O T R O R E M
I C I P E T E R K F R L
N E U N F L T M E V I I
T Y F L N R R J E F F N
K E V I N Z A M E G A N
Z N O R Z Z U N V L L I
Z S O N D R A M K T A E
```

3

Suitcase Jumble

The McCallisters are trying to pack for their vacation, but all their things are mixed up! Help them out by unscrambling the words below. The clues will help you.

GITHAIBTNSU
(What you wear in the pool.)

_ _ _ _ _ _ _ _ _ _

CONUSBKL
(Protects you from sunburn.)

_ _ _ _ _ _ _ _

NESASGLSUS
(Shady specs.)

_ _ _ _ _ _ _ _ _ _

HECABWELOT
(Great for lying on the sand.)

_ _ _ _ _ _ _ _ _ _

SSOTRH
(Pants for hot weather.)

_ _ _ _ _ _

BHACELALB
(This is fun to toss around.)

_ _○_ _ _ _ _ _

LASDANS
(Cool shoes.)

_ _ _ _ _○_ _

EPATLYREPA
(Brings music wherever you go.)

_ _ _ _ _○_ _ _ _

DACOMCERR
(Small video camera.)

_○_ _ _ _ _ _ _

HIRSTST
(Short-sleeved tops.)

_ - _ _ _ _ _○

Now unscramble the circled letters to find out where the McCallisters plan to spend Christmas Day. We've filled in the first letter of each word for you.

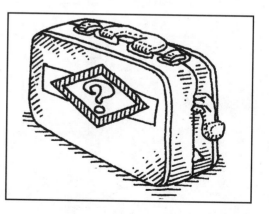

A _   T _ _   B _ _ _ _ _

5

Jailbreak Maze

Harry and Marv have broken out of jail!
Can you find their escape route?

START

ESCAPED

HARRY
8307-921

MARVIN
3654-260

FINISH

Airport Kriss Kross

Kevin and his family have made it to the airport at last! Can you fit all these airport words into the puzzle? We've filled in one to get you started.

4 letters
GATE
TAXI

6 letters
FLIGHT
RUNWAY

7 letters
BAGGAGE
SHUTTLE
TICKETS

8 letters
AIRPLANE
BOARDING

9 letters
CAFETERIA
PASSENGER

BAGGAGE

The Wrong Man

Kevin's father is wearing a trench coat – but so are a lot of other men at the airport. Which of these men is slightly different from the others?

Secret Landing

Where will Kevin's plane land?

To find out, use the secret code.

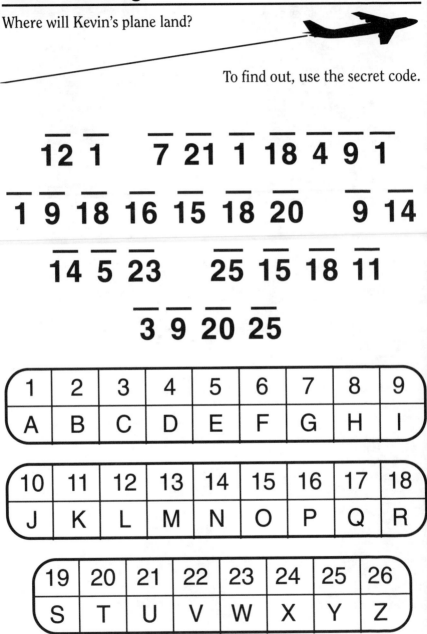

$\overline{12}\ \overline{1}$ $\overline{7}\ \overline{21}\ \overline{1}\ \overline{18}\ \overline{4}\ \overline{9}\ \overline{1}$

$\overline{1}\ \overline{9}\ \overline{18}\ \overline{16}\ \overline{15}\ \overline{18}\ \overline{20}$ $\overline{9}\ \overline{14}$

$\overline{14}\ \overline{5}\ \overline{23}$ $\overline{25}\ \overline{15}\ \overline{18}\ \overline{11}$

$\overline{3}\ \overline{9}\ \overline{20}\ \overline{25}$

1	2	3	4	5	6	7	8	9
A	B	C	D	E	F	G	H	I

10	11	12	13	14	15	16	17	18
J	K	L	M	N	O	P	Q	R

19	20	21	22	23	24	25	26
S	T	U	V	W	X	Y	Z

Whose Is Whose?

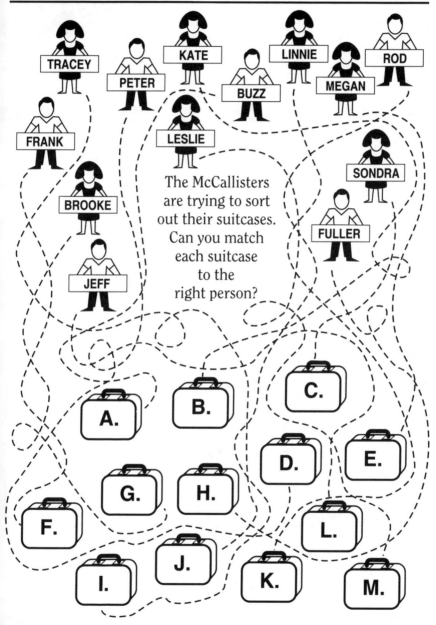

The McCallisters are trying to sort out their suitcases. Can you match each suitcase to the right person?

Scrambled Sights

There are lots of things to see in New York City.
Unscramble the names of these famous places
and match them to their descriptions.

1. DOWRL EDTAR NETCRE

2. PERIEM TTSAE LUIGBIND

3. SMETI QASERU

4. TENCLAR APKR

5. UUSMEM FO LARANUT
TYSOHRI

6. FOLREKLECRE TRENEC

7. USAETT FO YERILTB

8. DENITU STANNIO

a. This famous theater area is lit up by huge neon signs.

b. This museum has a room full of dinosaurs.

c. These twin towers are the second-tallest buildings in the world.

d. You'll find a tall Christmas tree and lots of ice skaters here.

e. In the classic movie, King Kong climbed this famous building.

f . World leaders meet here.

g. Here you'll find a zoo, gardens, a lake, and lots of room for picnics and ball games.

h. This lady stands tall in New York Harbor.

1. _____ matches letter _____
2. _____ matches letter _____
3. _____ matches letter _____
4. _____ matches letter _____
5. _____ matches letter _____
6. _____ matches letter _____
7. _____ matches letter _____
8. _____ matches letter _____

Skyline Maze

The New York City skyline is quite a sight! Can you find your way through this sky-high maze?

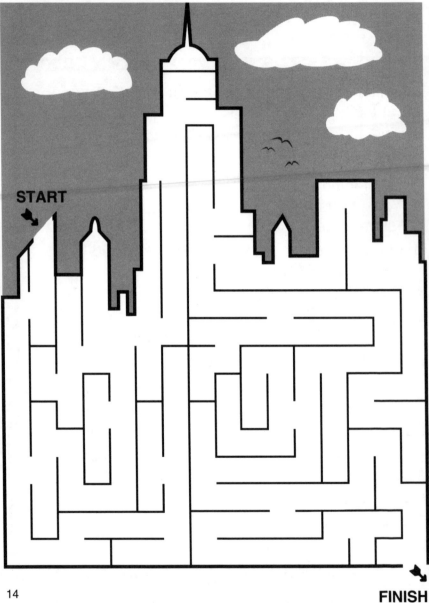

START

FINISH

Market Hideout

Harry and Marv are hiding in the food market.
Can you find them?

Hotel Crossword

Kevin is staying at the Plaza Hotel. Use these clues about hotels to solve the puzzle.

ACROSS:

1. The large room at the entrance of the hotel is called a _____.

4. To unlock the door, you need a _____.

5. You will be in trouble if you don't pay your _____ before you leave!

6. You can call _____ _____ and have dinner brought to your room.

7. When you arrive at the hotel, you must go to the front desk and _____ _____.

9. You can have breakfast, lunch, or dinner in the hotel _____.

11. It's fun to swim in the hotel _____.

DOWN

2. If you have a lot of suitcases, the _____ will carry them to your room.

3. If the hotel is saving a room for you, you have a _____.

8. If your room is on the top floor, you can take the _____ instead of the stairs.

10. Money you give to people who wait on you is called a _____.

Traveling Rebus

What's one way Kevin gets around New York? Solve the puzzle to find out.

_ _ _ _ _ _ _ _ _ _

Fun 'n' Games Word Search

Duncan's Toy Chest is crammed with toys! Can you find all these toys in the puzzle? Look across, up and down, and diagonally.

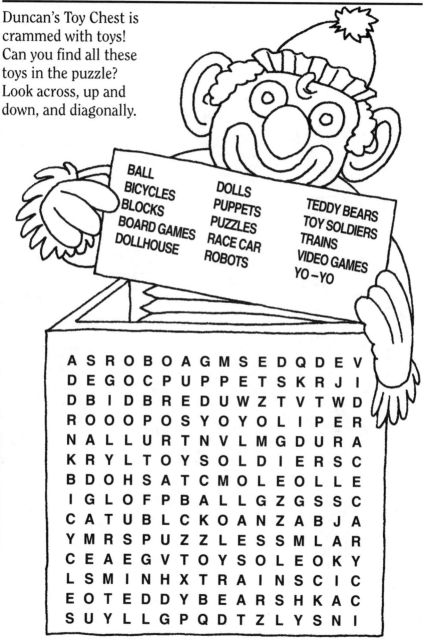

BALL
BICYCLES
BLOCKS
BOARD GAMES
DOLLHOUSE
DOLLS
PUPPETS
PUZZLES
RACE CAR
ROBOTS
TEDDY BEARS
TOY SOLDIERS
TRAINS
VIDEO GAMES
YO – YO

```
A S R O B O A G M S E D Q D E V
D E G O C P U P P E T S K R J I
D B I D B R E D U W Z T V T W D
R O O O P O S Y O Y O L I P E R
N A L L U R T N V L M G D U R A
K R Y L T O Y S O L D I E R S C
B D O H S A T C M O L E O L L E
I G L O F P B A L L G Z G S S C
C A T U B L C K O A N Z A B J A
Y M R S P U Z Z L E S S M L A R
C E A E G V T O Y S O L E O K Y
L S M I N H X T R A I N S C I C
E O T E D D Y B E A R S H K A C
S U Y L L G P Q D T Z L Y S N I
```

What a Mess!

Someone's mixed things up at Duncan's Toy Chest. Can you find at least 13 things wrong with this picture?

Where Are They?

Harry and Marv are hiding in Duncan's Toy Chest.
Use the secret code to figure out where they are.

R̄ M̄   Ḡ S̄ V̄

K̄ Ō Z̄ B̄ S̄ L̄ F̄ H̄ V̄

A = Z	
B = Y	
C = X	
D = W	
E = V	
F = U	
G = T	
H = S	
I = R	
J = Q	
K = P	
L = O	
M = N	

Match the Ornament

1.

A beautifully decorated Christmas tree stands in Duncan's Toy Chest. Can you spot the one and only ornament that exactly matches the one above?

2.

3.

4.

5.

6.

Trouble in Town

What's happening in this picture? Connect the dots to find out.

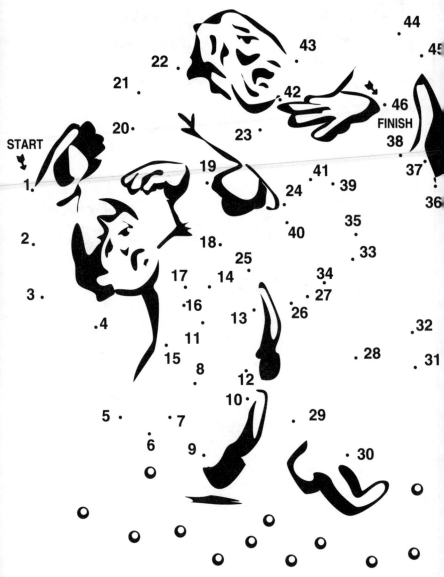

Connect the <u>letters</u> on this page.

Escape from the Hotel!

The hotel employees are after Kevin! Help him escape by finding the right path through the maze.

START

OUT OF ORDER

FINISH

Hidden in the Park

Kevin is hiding in Central Park. Lots of words are hiding there, too! How many words can you make from the letters in CENTRAL PARK? There are over 140!

_____

_____

_____

_____

_____

_____

_____

Lost Letter Maze

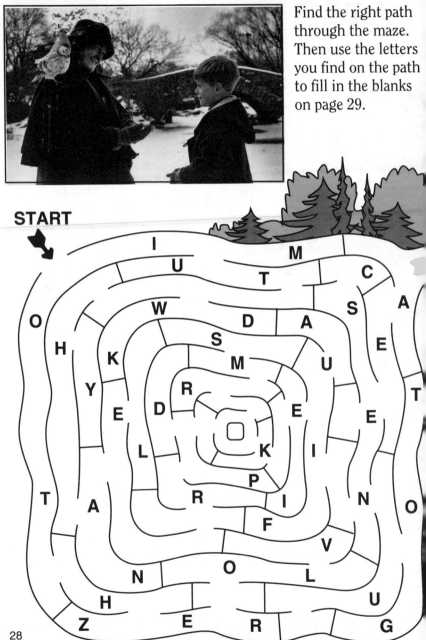

Find the right path through the maze. Then use the letters you find on the path to fill in the blanks on page 29.

START

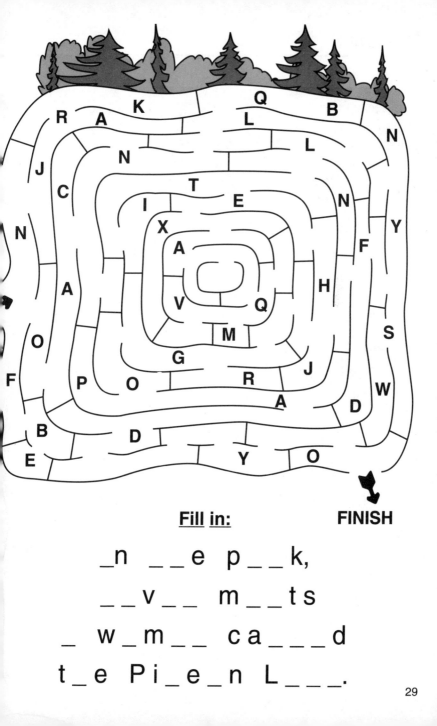

Fill in:

_n _ _ e p _ _ k,

_ _ v _ _ m _ _ t s

_ w _ m _ _ c a _ _ _ d

t _ e P i _ e _ n L _ _ _ .

Stop the Fight

Can you separate the cats and pigeons in the circle before there's trouble? Divide them by drawing just 3 straight lines, so each animal is by itself.

Where Is Kevin?

Kevin and the Pigeon Lady go to a famous place in New York City. The name of this place is hidden in the letters below. To find out what it is, cross out every other letter, starting with the first one. The letters that are left will spell out the answer.

G R C A X D O I Z

O Q C M I L T G Y

O M Q U H S M I T

C A H C A I L P L

Answer: _ _ _ _ _   _ _ _ _

_ _ _ _ _   _ _ _ _

Animal Kriss Kross

Central Park is full of pigeons. Lots of other animals live there, too. Here are some other animals you might find in a park. Try to fit all of them into the puzzle. We've filled in one word to get you started.

3 letters
CAT
FOX

4 letters
CROW
FROG

5 letters
ROBIN
SKUNK

6 letters
RABBIT
TURTLE

7 letters
OPOSSUM
RACCOON
SPARROW

8 letters
CARDINAL
CHIPMUNK
SQUIRREL

S
P
A
R
R
O
W

Battle Plan

Kevin has big plans for those terrible thieves, Harry and Marv! Where is he going to fight them? Solve the puzzle to find out.

War on Crime Word Search

Kevin needs a lot of things for Operation Ho! Ho! Ho! Help him find these items in the puzzle by looking across, up and down, and diagonally.

BUCKET
GLUE
HAMMER
KEROSENE
LADDER
NAILS
PAINT

ROPE
SAW
SCREWDRIVER
TOOLCHEST
TORCH
VARNISH
WRENCH

```
T A Q U X T O H A M M E R Y
O K E R O S E N E J A C Z A
O K P R G V U E T L R S G L
C H G N O R A D O A D O D E
S V A L I S A R R B S C P W
A K E R U H N Y C D C H M E
W S O Z F E G E H E R I A R
I L N L J A F M E G E H L K
T O O L C H E S T I W J A L
V A D N F O P E C H D K D M
P W L V H N A I L S R N D O
R R K C A T Y N M A I Q E S
B E W W R R A P G X V U R N
T N T O O E N A N I E W R E
R C W X U V Y I A L R B R H
O H N H O R C N S P C L A D
P F B U C K E T C H Z H V Z
```

Kevin's Prize Jumble

Kevin has something that Harry and Marv don't want anyone else to see. To find out what Kevin has, first unscramble the words on page 37. The clues will help you.

LIRODAF
(State with lots of beaches.)

— — ⭕ — — ⭕

TRARIPO
(Place where planes come and go.)

— — — ⭕ — — —

TLEHO
(Place to stay on vacation.)

⭕ — — — —

NOELA
(By yourself.)

— — ⭕ — —

TSARCISHM
(December holiday.)

— — ⭕ — — — — — ⭕

NIPOSEG
(City birds.)

⭕ ⭕ — — — — —

OROYTEST
(Place to buy games and toys.)

— — — — ⭕ — ⭕ —

Now unscramble the circled letters to find out what Harry and Marv are after. We've filled in the first letter for you.

P — — — — — — — — — —

A Dangerous Maze

Harry and Marv are after Kevin! Lead them through the maze to Uncle Rob's house.

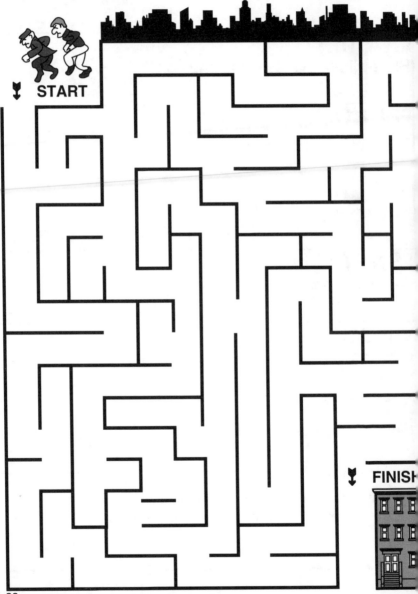

START

FINISH

Park Puzzler

What happens to Harry and Marv in the park? Use these clues to solve the puzzle and find out.

ACROSS:
1. Tosses.
3. Bird often found in parks and cities.
5. Another word for "those people."
6. Polite word for "woman."

DOWN:
1. One of the most common words in the English language.
2. What people feed birds.
4. Opposite of off.

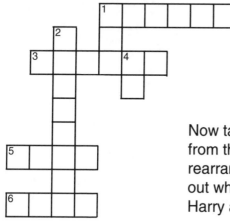

Now take all the words from the puzzle and rearrange them to find out what happened to Harry and Marv.

Answer:

_____

_____ .

39

Christmas Tree Maze

Kevin and his mother are heading to Rockefeller Center to meet
each other. Help Kevin and Kate find their way to the Christmas
tree by helping each one through the maze.

START

FINISH

FINISH

START

Dear Mr. Duncan...

Use the secret code to find out what Kevin wrote in his note to Mr. Duncan. Fill in each blank with the letter of the alphabet that comes <u>after</u> the letter written below each blank. For example, the letter "S" becomes a "T."

<u>I</u>'<u>M</u> <u>S</u><u>O</u><u>R</u><u>R</u><u>Y</u>
H L R N Q Q X

<u>I</u> <u>B</u><u>R</u><u>O</u><u>K</u><u>E</u>
H A Q N J D

<u>Y</u><u>O</u><u>U</u><u>R</u>
X N T Q

<u>W</u><u>I</u><u>N</u><u>D</u><u>O</u><u>W</u>.
V H M C N V

Holiday Hide-and-Seek

It's Christmas morning!
There are presents for
all the McCallisters.
Can you find all 14
packages in the picture?

ANSWERS

Page 3

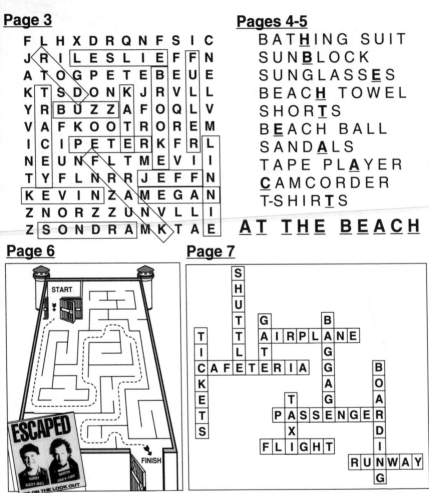

```
F L H X D R Q N F S I C
J R I L E S L I E F F N
A T O G P E T E B E U E
K T S D O N K J R V L L
Y R B U Z Z A F O Q L V
V A F K O O T R O R E M
I C I P E T E R K F R L
N E U N F L T M E V I I
T Y F L N R R J E F F N
K E V I N Z A M E G A N
Z N O R Z Z U N V L L I
Z S O N D R A M K T A E
```

Pages 4-5

B A T **H** I N G   S U I T
S U N **B** L O C K
S U N G L A S S **E** S
B E A C **H**   T O W E L
S H O R T **S**
B **E** A C H   B A L L
S A N D **A** L S
T A P E   P L **A** Y E R
C A M C O R D E R
T - S H I R T **S**

A T   T H E   B E A C H

Page 6

Page 7

Pages 8-9 Number **3** is different.

Page 10

LA GUARDIA AIRPORT IN NEW YORK CITY

Page 11

A. belongs to Buzz.

B. belongs to Kate.

C. belongs to Sondra.

D. belongs to Peter.

E. belongs to Megan.

F. belongs to Frank.

G. belongs to Brooke.

H. belongs to Fuller.

I. belongs to Rod.

J. belongs to Tracey.

K. belongs to Linnie.

L. belongs to Jeff.

M. belongs to Leslie.

Pages 12-13

1. **(c.)** WORLD TRADE CENTER
2. **(e.)** EMPIRE STATE BUILDING
3. **(a.)** TIMES SQUARE
4. **(g.)** CENTRAL PARK
5. **(b.)** MUSEUM OF
          NATURAL HISTORY
6. **(d.)** ROCKEFELLER CENTER
7. **(h.)** STATUE OF LIBERTY
8. **(f.)** UNITED NATIONS

Page 14

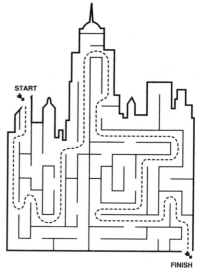

START

FINISH

Page 15

Page 18

LIMOUSINE

Pages 16-17

45

```
A S R O B O A G M S E D Q D E V
D E G O C P U P P E T S K R J I
D B I D B R E D U W Z T V T W D
R O O O P O S Y O Y O L I P E R
N A L L U R T N V L M G D U R A
K R Y L T O Y S O L D I E R S C
B D O H S A T C M O L E O L L E
I G L O F P B A L L G Z G S S C
C A T U B L C K O A N Z A B J A
Y M R S P U Z Z L E S S M L A R
C E A E G V T O Y S O L E O K Y
L S M I N H X T R A I N S C I C
E O T E D D Y B E A R S H K A C
S U Y L L G P Q D T Z L Y S N I
```

Page 22
IN THE PLAYHOUSE

Page 23
Number **5** is the matching ornament.

Page 26

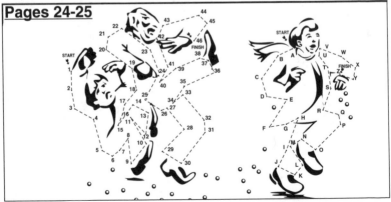

Pages 20-21

Pages 24-25

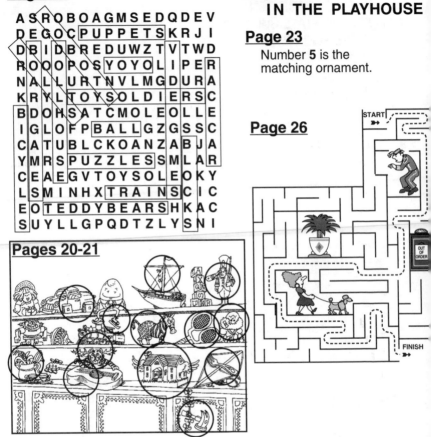

Page 27

ace, acre, act, ale, altar, alter, ant, ante, ape, arc, are, area, ark, art, ate, cake, can, canal, cane, canter, cap, cape, caper, car, care, caret, cart, carter, cat, cater, cent, central, clan, clap, clear, crane, crank, crate, creak, ear, earl, earn, eat, elk, enact, kale, lace, lack, lake, lance, lancer, lane, lank, lap, lark, late, later, leak, lean, leap, learn, lent, let, nap, nape, neap, near, neat, neck, net, pace, pacer, pack, packer, pact, pal, pale, paler, pan, pane, panel, pant, par, pare, parent, park, part, partner, pat, pate, pea, peak, peal, pear, pearl, peat, pecan, pelt, pen, pent, pet, petal, plan, plane, plank, plant, planter, prance, prancer, prank, race, racer, rack, rake, ran, rank, rant, ranter, rap, rare, rat, rate, react, real, reap, rear, recant, rent, tack, tale, talk, talker, tan, tank, tanker, tap, tape, tar, tare, tea, teak, teal, tear, ten, trace, tracer, track, tracker, trance, trap.

Page 30

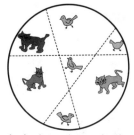

Pages 28-29

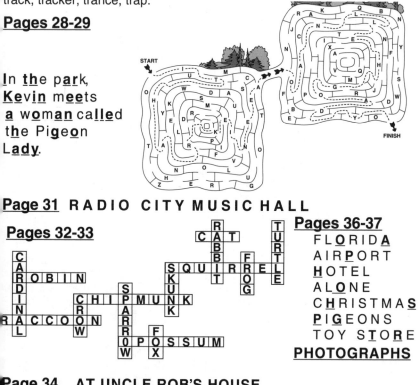

In **the** p**ar**k, **Kevin** mee**t**s **a** w**o**m**an** cal**ll**ed t**h**e Pige**o**n L**ady**.

Page 31 RADIO CITY MUSIC HALL

Pages 32-33

(crossword puzzle)

CARDINAL
ROBIN
CHIPMUNK
RACCOON
CAT
RABBIT
SQUIRREL
SKUNK
FROG
TURTLE
SPARROW
FOX
OPOSSUM

Pages 36-37

FL**O**RID**A**
AIR**P**ORT
HOTEL
AL**O**NE
C**H**RISTMA**S**
PI**G**EONS
TOY S**T**O**R**E
PHOTOGRAPHS

Page 34   AT UNCLE ROB'S HOUSE.

Page 35 answer on following page.

Page 35

```
T A Q U X T O H A M M E R Y
O K E R O S E N E J A C Z A
O K P R G V U E T L R S G L
C H G N O R A D O A D O D E
S V A L I S A R R B S C P W
A K E R U H N Y C D C H M E
W S O Z F E G E H E R I A R
I L N L J A F M E G E H L R K
T O O L C H E S T I W J A L M
V A D N F O P E C H D K D D O
P W L V H N A I L S R N D S N
R R K C A T Y N M A I Q E S N
B E W W R R A P G X V U R N E
T N T O O E N A N I E W R E
R C W X U V Y I A L R B R H
O H N H O R C N S P C L A D
P F B U C K E T C H Z H V Z
```

Page 38

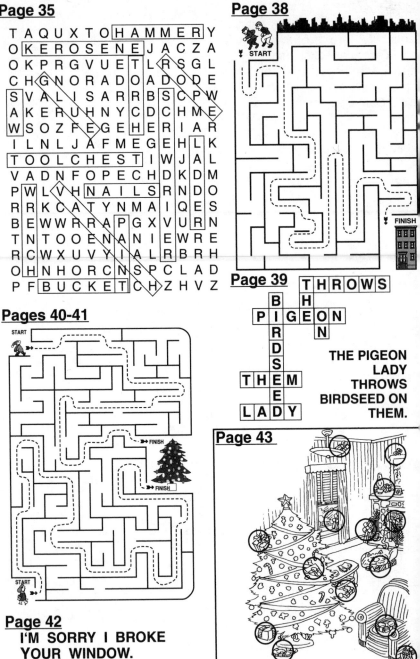

Page 39

```
        T H R O W S
      B   H
  P I G E O N
      R   N
      D
      S
T H E M
      E
L A D Y
```

THE PIGEON LADY THROWS BIRDSEED ON THEM.

Pages 40-41

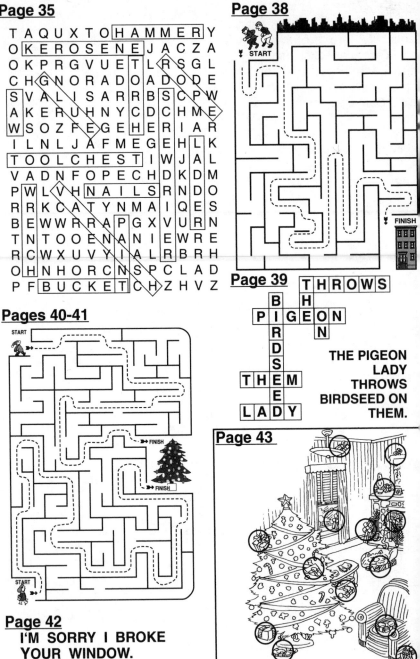

Page 42

I'M SORRY I BROKE YOUR WINDOW.

Page 43

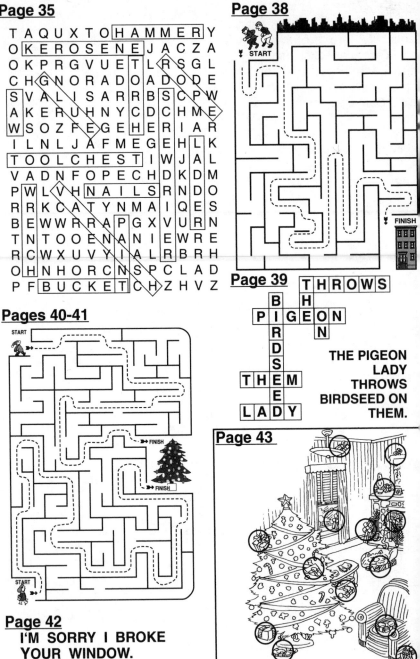

48